**"Where were you, Kim?" Coach Diaz shouted.**

"I don't know. I just—"

"You can't let anyone get past you like that. You have to keep your body between her and the goal."

Kim knew that. She walked back, with her hands on her hips. Soccer was like basketball, in a way, but the field was so much bigger. There was always more territory to cover. It wasn't as easy to stay tight on the player she was defending.

"Okay. Let's try it again," the coach yelled. "Same players."

So Kim got ready again. But that's when she heard one of the girls who was watching on the sidelines. "Kim's not going to be a star at this sport," the girl said. "I don't think she's going to last."

# BACKUP SOCCER STAR

## by Dean Hughes

Bullseye Books 🏠 Random House

New York

A BULLSEYE BOOK PUBLISHED BY RANDOM HOUSE, INC.

Text copyright © 1995 by Dean Hughes
Cover illustration copyright © 1995 by Dennis Lyall

*Library of Congress Cataloging-in-Publication Data*
Hughes, Dean, 1943–
Backup soccer star /by Dean Hughes
p.  cm.
SUMMARY: Thirteen-year-old Kim is a star in softball, basketball, and
volleyball, but when she begins playing soccer she fears she will let
the team down.
ISBN 0-679-85442-8 (pbk.) — ISBN 0-679-95442-2 (lib. bdg.)
[1. Soccer—Fiction.] I. Title.
PZ7. H87312Baf  1995
[Fic]—dc20
94-15128
RL: 4.7
First Bullseye Books edition: April 1995
Manufactured in the United States of America  10 9 8 7 6 5 4 3 2 1

# CHAPTER 1

"Soccer? Kim, what are you thinking? Why do you want to play soccer?"

Kim McKay was caught in the middle. Two of her best friends were staring her in the face. It was Kelsie Wixom, from her softball team, who had asked the question. But it was Dawn Alvarez, from her soccer team, who answered.

"What's wrong with soccer?" Dawn asked, turning toward Kelsie. "Kim's going to be good at it."

"It's softball season! That's what's wrong with it," Kelsie told Dawn.

"So what? What's your problem? She can play both sports."

"*How?*" Kelsie practically shouted. "We practice almost every night. And we have games every week."

Kelsie and Dawn were almost nose-to-nose, both

seeming to forget that Kim was there.

"You don't have *real* practices every night," Dawn said. "Most of the time it's just a bunch of girls getting together to—"

"Wait a minute!" Kim interrupted.

Dawn and Kelsie stopped and looked back at her.

"I've thought this all through," Kim said. "I can play both sports. We only have one official practice a week for each sport—and one game."

"Have you told the coach?" Kelsie asked.

"Yes. And she said it was okay."

That was true—in a way. Kim had told the softball coach she planned to play both sports this spring. What Kim wasn't telling her friends was that the coach had not been happy about it. Kim was thirteen, and this would be her last year to play in the league she was in now. The coach really wanted Kim's full attention on softball.

Kim and Kelsie played in a softball league in Maryville, Texas, a suburb of Dallas. Kim had been the star shortstop on the team for two seasons. The team was a sure bet to win the championship. But the girls were hoping to do much more than that. They expected to do well at the state tournament in Austin this year—maybe even come home state champs.

Still, Kim's softball coach had finally said, "I can't stop you, Kim. I think you're making a mistake by playing on both teams, but you're old enough to make your own decisions."

That, of course, wasn't exactly a strong vote of confidence. But Kim hadn't mentioned it to her friends on the softball team—especially Kelsie.

"Kim," Kelsie said, obviously trying to keep her voice calm, "you already play volleyball and basketball—besides softball. You can't do *everything*."

"I know that."

"She's fantastic at every sport," Dawn said. "She doesn't have to practice softball. She's already your best player."

Kelsie glanced over—and down—at Dawn, and gave her a look of disgust. Kelsie was a tall girl, a first baseman, with light brown hair that always sunbleached to blond in the summer. Dawn was petite by comparison. But she didn't back away. Her dark eyes, usually pretty and soft, were set firm.

"*Everyone* on the softball team has to practice hard this year. We want to take state," Kelsie said, almost growling.

"Well, so do we!" Dawn answered, her voice rising to a little shriek.

"Wait a minute!" Kim said as she grabbed both her friends by the shoulder. "Back off! Both of you."

The two girls did step away from each other a little, and they looked at Kim.

"I'm playing softball *and* soccer. I'm sorry,

3

Kelsie, but that's the way it is. And right now Dawn and I have to get to soccer practice. I'll see you at softball practice tomorrow night."

"This is so stupid," Kelsie mumbled, but she turned and walked away, taking long strides. She was wearing her cream-colored softball shorts, and she seemed all legs.

Kim and Dawn, both wearing their Striders uniforms—light blue with silver stripes—watched her for a moment. Then the two of them headed off to practice. Dawn shook her head and said, "Kelsie is so stupid."

But Kim didn't like that. "No, she isn't. The truth is, I never should have let you talk me into playing soccer. I really don't have the time to do both."

"Then quit softball."

"I can't do that, Dawn. I love softball. And Kelsie's right. We do have a chance at state this year. Really, I should just drop out of soccer before the first game."

"Come on, Kim. You promised."

Kim told herself that was the whole point. It's true that she had always wanted to play soccer on a real team—not just in gym class—but the main thing was, she had promised. Not only had she told her best friend, Dawn, that she would play, but she had promised all the girls on the soccer team—and the coach. But now she was wondering whether she had done the right thing.

* * *

Soccer, Kim had already learned, was harder than any sport she had ever played—even basketball. At practice the coach kept the girls running just about all the time. And the skills were really strange to Kim. Her impulse was to use her hands, and even though she was probably the best athlete on the team, she was having trouble learning to control the ball with her feet and body.

She knew she could do it, though. She had been the star of every sport she had ever played, and she always picked things up very quickly. She had grown up playing sports with her two big brothers, and they had always pushed her to the limit. She loved to compete, and she loved the feeling that she could dominate any sport she learned.

But her first real lesson came that night at practice, when Maria Diaz, the coach, set up some three-on-three drills and asked Kim to play defense. Coach Diaz had grown up in Mexico, and she had played soccer there. She knew the game well, and she expected a lot out of the girls.

Kim was suddenly standing face-to-face with Crystal Barker, one of the best players on the team. The girl lived for soccer.

Crystal was fairly small and stout, and she didn't have Kim's open-field speed. But she could move like a jackal, with amazingly quick moves in any direction. When Kim watched Crystal run with the ball, the ball seemed to be attached to Crystal's shoe with a rubber band. But when Crystal fired a shot, there was no doubt that the ball was free to fly.

Kim was taller than Crystal, with long, powerful legs. And she was a striking girl, with huge eyes like green plums and red hair cut short and straight just below her ears. She looked like an athlete, even when she was standing still. But that was the problem. Crystal had the moves to leave her doing exactly that—just standing there.

Kim bent forward a little, with her feet set rather wide apart. She waited and watched for Crystal to make a move. But Crystal used the inside of her foot to kick the ball over to Shawndra Cooper, the only black girl on the team. Shawndra was a quiet but tough little girl who usually played fullback.

Kim glanced to see where the ball was going. In that instant, Crystal broke inside Kim and dashed for the goal. Shawndra volleyed the ball directly back to Crystal, and Crystal drove straight at the goal.

Kim dashed with her and made up the distance quickly. But just as Kim was getting in position to cut her off, Crystal slammed a low, hard shot at the corner of the goal.

Franny Nixon, the goalie, was frozen. She made a late dive, but by then the ball was already in the net.

"Where were you, Kim?" Coach Diaz shouted.

"I don't know. I just—"

"You can't let anyone get past you, close in like that. You have to keep your body between her and the goal."

Kim knew that. She walked back, with her hands on her hips. It was like basketball, in a way, but the field was so much bigger. There was always more territory to cover. It wasn't as easy to stay tight on the player she was defending.

"Okay. Let's try it again," the coach yelled. "Same players."

So Kim got ready again. But that's when she heard one of the girls who was watching on the sidelines. "Kim's not going to be a star at this sport," the girl said. "I don't think she's going to last."

Kim gave the girl, Allie Sorenson, a quick glance, just to let her know that she had heard. But she could see in Allie's face that Allie had meant for her to hear. Allie was a rugged-looking girl with strong shoulders and stocky legs.

Kim was ready, but now she was mad. This time Crystal wasn't getting past her. She was going to show Allie who the real athlete was.

Shawndra brought the ball toward the defense this time. She dropped it off to Heather North, on the left side.

Kim watched all this out of the corner of her

eye. But she never let Crystal out of her sight. She kept her body square, between Crystal and the goal.

Crystal ran to her left, toward the center of the field. Then she dropped back, away from Kim, to take a pass. Heather shot a low pass toward her, and Crystal controlled the ball with the inside of her foot.

She faced Kim.

She gave a couple of little head fakes, and then suddenly she swung her leg as though she were going to blast a pass back to Heather. But she stopped her foot short of the ball.

Kim took the fake and turned away.

That's when Crystal tapped the ball to her left. Then she darted to the ball and pushed it past Kim.

Kim recovered quickly and stabbed at the ball with her right foot. But that threw her off balance, which was all Crystal needed. She shot past Kim, took the ball in stride, and was on her way to the goal again.

This time Crystal missed the shot, lifting it a little too high. But it didn't matter. Kim heard some girls laugh, and she heard Allie say something to the girl standing next to her. She was keeping her voice softer this time, but Kim knew more or less what she was saying.

"Kim, you can't reach for the ball," the coach

said. "That's just exactly what a good dribbler like Crystal wants you to do. You have to cut her off with your body, not your leg."

Kim nodded. She knew that already. But it was a whole lot easier to understand than it was to do.

"Okay, six new girls," the coach shouted. "New attack team. New defense."

Allie ran onto the field, past Kim. Kim had no intention of saying anything to her. But Allie grinned, and Kim was suddenly furious. "I heard what you said," she told Allie.

Allie stopped. "I don't care. It's true. You think you can be the star of any team you play on. But you won't be the star on this team. It takes a long time to learn soccer."

"I'll outplay *you* before the year is over," Kim said. Then she walked off the field, straight to Dawn. Already, Kim knew she had done something dumb. "I shouldn't have told her that," she said.

"True," Dawn said, smiling, "but she did have it coming."

"Do you think I can do it?"

"Play better than Allie?"

"Yeah. This year."

"I don't know. She's pretty good."

That was not what Kim had wanted to hear.

9

# CHAPTER

## 2

For the next couple of weeks Kim practiced with both teams. In March the weather had started to warm up already, and Kim enjoyed being outside every night after school. She liked going hard, trying to do her best, and she liked being around the other girls—or at least most of them.

Yet she wasn't entirely comfortable with either team. All the softball players knew that Kim was playing soccer. Kelsie was the only one who had said anything about it, but Kim wondered what the others were thinking. These girls had been her good friends for years, and she didn't want them to think she was letting them down.

Something else was worrying her, too. She was fielding better than anyone else on the team—as always—and she was throwing bullets to first base. But she just wasn't hitting as well as she usually did.

The coach kept telling Kim that she was dropping her left shoulder and swinging under the ball. Maybe so, but no matter how Kim concentrated, her swing felt wrong. She was hitting pop-ups and weak fly balls. That wasn't like Kim, who had led the team in batting the year before.

Still, she kept telling herself that she would find the groove by the time the first game came around. And she told Kelsie one night right after batting practice—when she had struggled more than ever with her swing.

Kelsie shrugged. "Yeah. Probably," she said.

"What's that supposed to mean?"

"Nothing."

But Erin Woodward was standing nearby. She said, "You would be hitting better by now if you were over here taking batting practice every night—the way we are."

So it wasn't just Kelsie. They had all been talking about it. Kim knew that for sure now, yet she couldn't really say much. She had a feeling they might be right. "Don't worry. I'll hit," Kim said. She got her glove and headed out to take some infield practice. But she was more worried than she let on.

Kim felt even more pressure on the soccer field. Most of the girls on the team played soccer and only soccer—both fall and spring. Kim could never stop by Dawn's house without finding her out in

11

her backyard juggling with the ball. Dawn could keep the ball in the air for several minutes at a time, hitting it with her thigh, her instep, her head. Or she would line up and take shots, trying to pound the ball at a fence post.

Kim knew what most of the girls on the team thought of her. To them, Kim was the girl who considered soccer "something extra"—something fun to do but not her first love.

And, of course, that was true. But why couldn't they accept it? Maybe she could help the team even if she didn't live and breathe soccer the way they did.

The first soccer match of the season came before the first softball game. It was only a practice match, not one that counted in the league standings, but it was the Striders' first chance to find out how good they were going to be—and Kim's chance to find out how well she could do. The opponents were from Dallas, and from what she had heard they were good.

The match was played on the Maryville field, just down the street from Kim's middle school. A hard thunderstorm had rolled through the area the day before, and the field was still rather soft. Not only that, but the heat had returned and the humidity was high. By the time Kim finished warming up, she was already feeling hot and winded.

But that turned out not to matter. When Coach

Diaz called out the starting lineup, Kim's name wasn't on the list. Dawn and Crystal were playing the middle forward spots, and Allie was at a midfield position, along with a girl named Anne Deichman. Anne was a cross-country runner and a track star. She had long, slender legs and good speed, once she got going, but she didn't have the quickness of Crystal or Dawn.

Heather North and Rachel Harris were on the wings. They were similar players—both rather small, and both great dribblers. But that's where the similarities ended. Heather was a soft-spoken girl with wheat-colored hair, and Rachel was a loudmouth, constantly shouting in her deep voice. Her short-cropped hair and her protruding teeth, wired with braces, reminded Kim of some sort of rodent.

Franny Nixon would be the goalie. She wasn't as tall as most goalies, but she had a lot of experience—and good instincts. Most important, she was very quick. She also watched her team's defense closely, and she wasn't afraid to bark out commands.

Kim had thought she might get called on to play fullback, but her defensive play during practice must not have looked good enough to the coach. Shawndra Cooper was playing fullback with Marsella Flores and Lorrie Gertner. Marsella was a good-sized girl without the speed of some of the

13

other Striders, but she played hard defense, never leaving the player she was marking. Lorrie seemed all legs and arms, and she usually looked awkward, but she played just as hard as Marsella and was just as effective.

The coach had little Pam Gilbert playing sweeper. She hardly looked old enough to be out on the field with some of the girls, but she darted about as quick as a kitten, and she never backed down from girls who looked much stronger.

For the first time in her life, Kim was on the bench. Except that there was no bench. She sat down close to the touchline and watched the Striders kick off.

It didn't take long to see that the Dallas team, the Shooters, loved to attack. They had a lot of speed, and they weren't afraid to take chances. They wore bright red uniforms, and all that flash seemed to fit their personalities. The first five or six minutes of the match were played mostly at the Striders' defensive end of the field.

A tall black girl named Tanya Sanders was the star forward for the Shooters, and she knew how to keep the pressure on the fullbacks. She broke free twice in the early going. Franny was quick enough to cut off the first shot, and Tanya was wide with her shot the second time.

But Kim knew the score could easily be 2 to 0 right now, and the Striders were lucky that it wasn't.

The Shooters, however, were taking chances on defense, and finally they took one chance too many. Heather had the ball near midfield and a defender came at her a little too fast. Heather faked to the left and cut to the right, and the defender, trying to reverse her direction, slipped on the soft turf.

The defender went down, and Heather broke upfield toward the Shooters' goal. Crystal was in front of her and couldn't take a pass without being called offside, but she slowed and moved toward the center of the field.

Heather kept dribbling until a fullback covered her, and then she flipped a pass over to Crystal.

Crystal hadn't had a chance to show what she could do yet, and she took her defender by surprise. She controlled the ball and tapped it ahead in one motion. Then she raced forward, pushing the ball ahead of her. She was suddenly past the defender, charging toward the goal.

Another fullback picked her up, and Crystal had to pull up, but she spotted Rachel angling in from the wing. She lifted a looping pass in her direction. Rachel leaped and headed the ball across the center of the field, in front of the goal.

Crystal darted inside, took the pass out of the air with the inside of her knee, dropped it on the grass, and *fired*.

The goalie leaped to her right and got a hand on

the ball, but the shot was a rocket. The ball bounced off the goalie's hand and into the net.

The Striders all ran to Crystal. Suddenly they were a screaming little mob, grabbing at each other and jumping up and down.

Watching all this from the sidelines was something strange and new to Kim. She didn't mind someone else getting the glory—making the goal. She had never been one to hog all the attention on a team. But what she couldn't stand was being a spectator. She might as well have been a cheerleader or somebody's mom.

Dawn ran to her position for the kickoff, but then she yelled to Kim, "We can beat these girls. They're not as good as they think they are."

"That's right!" Kim shouted back. She clapped her hands and tried to sound excited for the team. But she felt no part of any of this.

Kim took a long look at the coach, trying to tell her with her eyes that she wanted to play. But it didn't happen. The coach was sticking with the starting lineup for now.

A couple of minutes later, Tanya got open, and this time she didn't waste her chance. One of the Shooters' wings took a shot that Franny blocked, but the ball bounced loose toward the corner of the goal area.

Tanya got to the ball at the same time Lorrie did, but somehow Tanya managed to knock the ball loose, and then she pounced on it. She lashed a shot just inside the goalpost before Franny could even move.

So the score was 1 to 1, and Kim could see that things were going to stay tight. But it was hard for her to care the way she wanted to.

Then the coach yelled, "Kim, go in for Lorrie. Get on that tall forward of theirs—Tanya—and stay on her. You're as fast as she is, so make life miserable for her."

Now that was something Kim could understand—making life miserable for an opponent. She dashed onto the field and took up her position. She was going to shut down this Tanya girl.

Dawn yelled to her, "Okay, Kim, show her what you can do."

Kim nodded and clapped her hands. She had the very same thing in mind—except that Dawn probably meant Tanya, and Kim was thinking a little more about showing the coach what she could do. And somewhere in the back of her mind was the thought that she wouldn't mind showing Allie and some of the other girls on the team.

Just a few seconds later, Kim got her chance. The Shooters took control of the ball in the middle of the field and were suddenly on the attack again. One of the wings drove the ball hard down the touchline and then kicked a crossing pass.

Tanya raced to the ball with Kim right on her.

17

Tanya controlled the ball with her thigh and then spun and faced Kim. Kim stayed low and balanced, keeping her body between Tanya and the goal. She was ready for any move.

But Tanya dropped the ball back to another player. She walked a couple of steps to her right. And then—*pow*—she broke to the goal, leaving Kim in her tracks.

The midfielder who had taken the pass tried to loop the ball right back to Tanya. The pass was a little long, however, and Franny broke to the ball and caught it.

But if the pass had been right, Tanya would have had it in the open. And she would have scored.

Kim couldn't believe it. Soccer was a tough game.

Somewhere, not far away, Allie was yelling, "Kim, you can't let her get away from you like that."

"I know," Kim said, mostly to herself. But she didn't have time to think about it. Tanya was trying to get open again.

# CHAPTER

## 3

Kim thought only of defense—only of Tanya. She stayed on the girl tight, no matter where she went. And Tanya knew all the tricks. When someone would knock the ball out of bounds, Tanya would put her hands on her knees, bend over, and draw in long breaths as though she were exhausted. But then suddenly, as a player tossed the ball in, she would dash away.

Kim had never run so hard in her life. She was gasping for breath most of the time, but she didn't let Tanya get another open shot.

The only problem was, the Striders were not getting open, either. At one point, Rachel Harris made a great pass to Dawn, and Dawn blasted a header at the goal. But the Shooters' goalie reacted quickly and knocked the ball away. And that was as close as the Striders got.

More and more, the match was being fought in the middle of the field. Both defenses were hanging tough, battling back and forth, giving each other very few chances to shoot.

When halftime came, Kim trudged to the side of the field and sat down. Coach Diaz patted her on the shoulder. "Kim, good work on defense," she said. "I'm going to put Lorrie back in when the second half starts. But we'll split the time. That Tanya can wear you out, can't she?"

"I can deal with her," Kim said. She didn't want to be taken out. She still wanted to prove something to Tanya and to her team. She wanted to keep the score tied until one of her teammates could get a goal and win the match.

Dawn sat down next to Kim. "Good job," she said. But then she flopped on her back. "This team really works you," she muttered.

Kim was just glad to know that she wasn't the only one who was tired. When she looked around, she saw that the girls' uniforms had turned dark blue from sweat and that all the girls looked beat. Their faces were flushed and their hair was matted to their sweaty foreheads.

The coach let the girls breathe for a few minutes, and then she talked about the second half. "You're playing tough defense," she told them, "but when you take control of the ball, you all have to switch quickly and go on the attack. Sometimes that first second after you get the ball is the time when you can make a break before the defense picks you up."

Then she talked to the forwards about their passing. "Crystal, you're trying to dribble too much. These girls are too quick for that. You have to keep the ball moving."

Kim was hardly paying attention. But then the coach said, "And Kim, I told you to play good defense, but you have to think about attack, too. You're hanging back too much, and that means Tanya is free to double on our midfielders."

Kim was taken by surprise. She knew the coach was right, but she had figured stopping Tanya was enough. The truth was, she was still a little nervous about handling the ball.

"Okay," Kim said, "I'll watch that." But she suddenly felt uncomfortable. She had never been a weakness on a team—someone who couldn't do everything that was needed. No coach had ever had to talk to her like that.

Dawn seemed to know what Kim was thinking. She leaned close and whispered, "You're doing great. All this stuff takes time to learn."

But even that seemed some sort of pat on the back for the poor benchwarmer who was doing her best, even if she wasn't as good as the starters. Kim's pride was hit hard, and she made up her mind that when she got back in the match she

21

would prove she could do something for the attack.

But the second half started as the first half had ended. Both defenses were playing tough. The players were spending all their time knocking the ball around in the center of the field.

The only difference was that Kim was now watching from the sidelines again.

Then, just when it seemed that no one would ever get off a shot, Tanya took the ball away from Anne in the middle of the field and blasted a long pass. One of the Shooters' wings jumped high and headed the ball toward the goal. A forward got to the ball ahead of Lorrie and passed back to Tanya, who was running hard down the field.

Tanya got doubled by Pam and Shawndra, and she lost the ball for a moment. But she ran it down and kicked it out to the left wing. By now the Striders' defense had dropped back, and the advantage was lost. But the wing worked herself open enough to send a high crossing pass toward the goal area.

Tanya tried to break to the ball, but Pam ran with her, stayed in front, and got a foot on the ball. The ball rolled toward Marsella, who was about to knock it back upfield when the Shooters' right wing came flying in and knocked it back across the goal area.

One of the Shooters' forwards was in the right place at the right time. She got to the ball and stabbed it at the net. Franny dove, but the ball was just beyond her reach.

The Shooters went crazy. They jumped all over their forward. From the side of the field, Kim could hear them shouting, "Now we're rolling. Let's put this one away." Then, as one of the Shooters' players ran up the field for the kickoff, Kim heard her say, "It shouldn't be that tough to score on this team. They're not that good."

Kim was a competitor. It was bad enough to hear an opponent say something like that, but it was worse to be standing on the side, unable to do anything about it.

Another few minutes went by before she got her chance. And when the coach did put Kim back in the game, the Striders' attack was looking pretty sad. The Shooters were the ones pushing the ball, getting into Strider territory, even getting some shots off. The Striders were holding their own on defense, but they weren't doing anything with the ball when they had the chance.

Kim's legs were fresh now, and she figured Tanya, who had played the whole match, had to be getting tired. And so she decided to make something happen—immediately. She went for the steal the first time she got the chance.

Tanya tried to dribble past her, and Kim's good

reactions worked for her. She stayed in front of Tanya and then shot her foot out and batted the ball off Tanya's shins. Marsella, who was close by, chased after the ball and then hit it upfield.

Kim remembered what the coach had said, so she charged toward midfield. The only problem was, a Shooter midfielder had taken control of the ball and the Shooters were already on attack again.

Kim hurried back and got tight on Tanya. And when one of the Shooters tried to kick a pass in Tanya's direction, it was Kim who hustled to the ball first and hammered a pass toward the touch-line, where she saw Allie open.

Again Kim charged upfield, feeling good. Tanya *was* tired, and Kim was making her look bad. Now Kim wanted to get in on the attack. The Striders needed to put some pressure on the Shooters' defense.

Allie made a short run down the touchline, until she got cut off. Heather ran toward her, and Allie tried to make the pass. But a Shooter fullback shot in and took control of the ball. For a moment, Kim thought she would have to drop back on defense, but Dawn ran to the fullback and made a sliding tackle.

The ball bounced free and then rolled toward the touchline. Kim had moved farther up the field than she ever had before, and now she saw her chance. She broke hard, running all out, showing the speed that made her so good at every sport she played. And she got to the ball before it rolled out of bounds. She turned and kicked it back toward Dawn.

Kim dropped back a little, not wanting to let Tanya get loose behind her, but she watched as Dawn shot a pass toward the goal area. Crystal was there, but so were two defenders.

All three players jumped high, but it was Crystal who hit the ball with her forehead and pushed it toward Rachel, who was breaking in from the right wing.

Rachel had a step on her defender, and she took a hard shot. But one of the Shooters' fullbacks had a good angle. She took a step to her left and got in front of the ball.

The ball flew like a missile and bounced off the fullback's shins, straight back toward Rachel.

Rachel tried to get another shot off, but her defender stepped in and knocked the ball away. It bounced across the center of the field, near the goal area.

A crowd of girls was moving in on the ball from several directions. Dawn and Crystal were both part of the crash. A couple of players went down. As Kim watched from midfield, she thought for a moment that any chance for a shot was gone.

But the ball rolled free, and Rachel was the one who got to it first. This time she was one-on-one with the goalie. She controlled the ball, turned, and blasted...

No. Rachel faked a shot, and the goalie dove to her left. Then Rachel slammed the ball to the goalie's right side and into the net.

The Striders had tied up the match, 2 to 2!

Kim ran all the way to the goal to get in on the celebration this time. She grabbed Rachel when she got the chance and shouted with the others. "We're going to get them now!" everyone was saying.

Kim felt wonderful. She knew that she had been part of the attack this time. She had done a couple of things right, and it had made a difference.

Dawn knew it, too. She grabbed Kim and shouted, above the chaos, "You got us moving. You ran down the ball when it was going out of bounds. Nice job, Kim!"

Kim was glad Dawn had noticed, and she hoped that Allie and some of the others had noticed, too.

But the match was still tied, not won, and Kim wasn't going to be satisfied until she did something more to get the win.

# CHAPTER

# 4

Coach Diaz yelled from the sidelines, "Three and a half minutes to go. Get on the attack. Let's get another one." But then she added, "But don't get sloppy on defense."

Kim wasn't so worried about Tanya anymore. She knew the truth now. Maybe Kim lacked some experience, but she could stay with this girl.

Kim's confidence was soaring, and it only increased when Tanya took a pass and came toward Kim, looking determined. Tanya tried a little head fake and then tried to break past her. But Kim sidestepped and cut her off. Tanya tripped and went down.

Tanya got up screaming for a foul, but the referee didn't see it that way. And Kim had already shot a pass to Anne, who was making a move up the center of the field. Kim took off, hoping to get in on the attack again.

Anne tried to get the ball to Allie but didn't get enough power in her kick. The pass rolled weakly across the middle of the field, and a Shooter mid-fielder cut it off.

The Shooters came back hard on attack, and Kim hustled to pick up Tanya. She knew that time was running out, and she had to make something happen right away.

And so she decoyed Tanya a little. She stayed a few steps back, just daring the Shooters to pass in Tanya's direction.

Then, when the pass did come, she shot toward the ball. It was a good move, but when the ball landed in front of her and she tried to block it, it bounced just over her foot and right to Tanya. Kim was out of position, and Tanya had room to work.

Tanya dribbled toward the goal as Shawndra moved up to stop her. But Kim caught up quickly, and she and Shawndra forced Tanya outside. The Striders were getting back, and Tanya had nowhere to go with the ball.

She faded back a little, looking for someone to pass to. Then, suddenly, she struck. She feinted to the left and got Kim to lean that way, and then— *bam*—she knocked the ball past Kim on the right.

Tanya broke past her in the same instant, and Kim slipped on the soft ground as she tried to recover.

Kim didn't go down, but she lost a step. And that was all Tanya needed. She burst toward the goal. She dribbled once, twice, and then, just as Franny decided to charge her, Tanya drove a hard shot.

The ball was past Franny before she could react. And now the Shooters were the ones celebrating.

Kim couldn't believe what had happened. Tanya had seemed so tired, so finished. And then she had made that catlike move and was gone.

And now the time was almost gone, too. The last couple of minutes, the Shooters packed in on defense and gave the Striders no chance at all to shoot at the goal.

And then it was all over.

Tanya had been silent all through the match, but once it was over she walked up to Kim. "Good game," she said. "You played me tough."

But it was a little too generous. It only made Kim feel worse. She knew what had really happened. She had played all right at times, but she hadn't been up to Tanya at the moment of truth.

Kim walked to the sidelines and stood by herself. She could see how much this loss—even though it wasn't a league match—meant to the girls. They had a lot of pride, and they weren't used to losing, not to anyone. What Kim didn't know was whether or not they were blaming her.

When Dawn walked over to her, Kim said, "I'm sorry. I blew it."

"No. Tanya can make anyone look bad," Dawn said.

But Kim didn't want to hear that she had looked bad. In softball games, she had come up to bat needing to get a hit to win a game, and sometimes she had failed. She had also once missed a foul shot that could have won a big basketball game.

Yet it wasn't the same this time. In those games, she was the main reason the scores had been close in the first place. She almost always drove in the most runs for her softball team and scored the most points for her basketball team.

"Kim, don't take it so hard," Dawn whispered. "You were tough on Tanya most of the time."

Kim tried to think about it that way. But then she heard Allie. She was standing by Crystal, and she made no attempt to keep her voice down. "I wish Lorrie had been in there at the end. At least maybe we could have saved the tie."

Crystal spun and looked at Kim, then back at Allie. "Hey, don't say that," she said. "That's not fair."

Allie took a look at Kim, then looked away. She didn't say anything more, but she didn't take the words back, either.

When Kim got to her house after the match, she was glad to see that no one was home. But soon her parents came in together, and her dad walked upstairs to her room. The door was open, and Kim heard him come in, but she was sitting at her desk studying—or at least pretending to—and she didn't turn around.

"How did the game go, honey?"

Kim continued to look at her history book. "We lost," she said.

"Did you get to play much?"

"Yeah. Some."

"What's wrong?"

"Nothing, Dad. I've just got a lot of studying to do." She still wouldn't look at him.

Dad walked up close and then leaned around so that his face was almost touching hers. "Kimberly, come on. What's the matter?"

Kim sat back in her chair and looked at her dad. He was a tall man, but he was still bent toward her now. Kim wanted to be mad at him, but something in his gentle green eyes—eyes just like her own—said that he really was concerned.

"I just had a bad game. It's no big deal."

"What do you mean, a bad game?"

"I let a girl score—right at the end. And the other team beat us by that one goal."

"Kimberly, this is the first time you've played soccer. What can you expect?"

Kim didn't answer for a time. She didn't want to seem like a crybaby about the whole thing. Finally she said, "The coach asked me to stop one particular girl from scoring. But I couldn't do it."

Dad backed away and sat on Kim's bed. She could see him going into his counseling style. He was an assistant principal at a high school, and he spent a lot of time talking to kids. His tie was hanging loose, but now he took his glasses off and leaned forward. "I thought it was just a practice game," he said.

"It was."

"Well, the coach was letting you get some experience. And you got some. It shouldn't be anything to feel all that bad about. You're just learning the game."

"Dad, I know all that. I'm okay. I just feel kind of bad."

"Well, sure. You've never liked to lose. You're just like your brothers."

That was true. Kim's brothers were away at college now, but the three had always competed fiercely. Still, that wasn't the whole story. Kim didn't want to tell the rest, especially what Allie had said. "I know. I'm all right."

Dad nodded. And he thought for a time. Finally he said, "Maybe it's good for you to have to struggle with a sport that you can't dominate right from the beginning."

Kim thought her dad meant well, but somehow he sounded a little too much like Allie. The superstar needed to be humbled. Kim didn't think she had ever acted like a big shot just because she was good at sports.

Dad got up and gave Kim a little pat on the shoulder. "Hang in there, kid," he said. "You're going to learn some things."

Once her dad was gone, Kim shut her history book. She didn't really feel like studying. She lay down on her bed, with its brightly flowered bedspread, and then picked up her phone and called Kelsie—someone who would understand.

Kelsie listened to the whole story and then said, "I can't believe that Allie. She's such a little witch. Soccer is the only sport she plays, and she's not even *that* good at it."

"Actually, she *is* good," Kim said. "But I think she hates me. I don't know why. I've never bragged around her or anything like that."

"Kim, you're the best athlete in the whole school. And you *never* brag. Allie's just jealous. Think about it. To her, you're moving in on her territory—the one sport she's good at. The problem isn't with you. It's with her."

Kim really didn't think she had a big head, and she suspected Kelsie was right about Allie, but she only said, "All that doesn't really matter that much. I just feel rotten about being the one who lost the game."

There was a short silence on the line, and then Kelsie said, "Kim, face the facts. You don't have time enough to practice *every* sport. If you wanted to, you could be a great soccer player. But why? You're already so good at softball and basketball and volleyball. Why don't you just concentrate on those?"

"I can't quit now."

"Why not? It's still preseason, and you're not in the starting lineup. It won't hurt them that much if you quit. And I know you'll do better at softball if you aren't dividing up your practice time."

"I don't know, Kelsie. I need to think about it."

After Kim hung up the phone, she did think about it.

It took a while to come to the conclusion, but she finally made up her mind. She was going to tell Coach Diaz that she didn't have time to play soccer. It just wasn't worth it to her.

# CHAPTER 5

Kim knew she had to tell her parents that she was quitting soccer, but she kept putting it off. Part of the reason was that over the weekend she changed her mind about ten times. She talked to Kelsie a lot—and avoided Dawn. Finally she made up her mind that Kelsie was right. If she gave all her attention to one sport, she would play better. And the soccer team didn't really need her anyway.

The only problem was that Dawn was going to be very disappointed. Maybe even angry. So Kim waited to say anything until Tuesday, the day of soccer practice.

After school Kim walked over to the coach's house. When Coach Diaz answered the door, Kim asked if she could talk to her, and the two of them walked into the living room and sat down. Kim sat in a big chair, and the coach sat down on the couch across from her. The coach's two-year-old son, Nathan, climbed onto the couch next to his mom and kept smiling at Kim. That only made her feel worse about what she was going to do.

Kim just wanted to say what she had to say and have it over with. "Coach, I've decided to quit. I don't really have time to play soccer *and* softball, and I'm better at softball."

The coach nodded. She didn't seem surprised. She calmly asked, "Does this have anything to do with the match last Thursday?"

"Well, no. Not really."

"What does 'not really' mean?"

"I just...think I'll play better if I stick with one sport." Kim looked down at a little area rug under her feet.

"Why did you try out for soccer then?"

When Kim finally looked up, Coach Diaz's quiet, dark eyes focused on her own. Kim had the feeling she understood more than Kim wanted her to know. "I shouldn't have gone out, I guess. But Dawn wanted me to. I thought it would be fun. I didn't realize what a hard sport it is to learn."

"I've never seen *anyone* pick up soccer skills as fast as you have, Kim."

"Really?"

"Yes, really. And if you feel bad about that goal in that first match, forget it. You were up against one of the best players we're going to face all year."

36

"Well, it's not just that."

"It's also what Allie said, isn't it?"

Kim didn't know the coach had heard that. "Uh...maybe a little. But mainly I've just been thinking it all over, and I don't have the time. I really knew, before I tried out, that I probably shouldn't. I kept thinking I could work it out somehow."

"That's fine, Kim—if that's what you want to do. But I want you to think about a couple of things."

The coach sat quietly for a moment, still looking into Kim's eyes. She had her arm around Nathan, who had the same intense, dark brown eyes that his mom had. Kim found herself looking down at the floor again.

"Kim, maybe you shouldn't have gone out for both sports, but you did. And the reason you made our team is that I saw your athletic ability—your speed and your body control. I chose you over some girls who have played more because I knew that you would keep getting better all season. Right now, though, you're way ahead of anything I expected from you."

"Thanks," Kim said, and she wondered again whether quitting was the right thing to do.

"And here's the other thing you need to think about. I need girls like Crystal and Dawn. But I also need girls who can come into a match, give the starters a rest, and still keep up our intensity.

That's why I wanted you, Kim. I knew you had a lot to learn, but I could see you were such a competitor that you would play hard—and make up for your lack of experience."

"That's what I thought, too. But Thursday I just couldn't get the job done."

"Kim, on defense you played very well. A lot of defense is good athletic ability and reaction. It's not that different from basketball. You don't offer us great attack skills yet, but you can come in and play, and I know we don't have to be scared we'll give up an easy goal."

Kim was thinking now. She wasn't sure what to say. Suddenly she wasn't sure why—exactly—she had wanted to quit, but she suspected it wasn't for any of the reasons she had given herself.

"If you quit now," Coach Diaz continued, "it's going to hurt our team. I can't find another girl who can offer us what you can. But if you stay, you have to settle for the idea that you're a substitute, not a star. And you've always been a star before."

"I don't think of myself that way, Coach. I just play hard. At all sports. I don't have a big head or anything, no matter what Allie thinks."

"Maybe not. But I think maybe you can't handle being on the second team."

"No, it isn't that. Really. What I can't handle is

causing my team to lose. I've never done that before."

The coach laughed. "First of all, there's no such thing. Soccer is a *team* sport. No one player ever wins or loses a match. The amazing thing to me is that I threw you into a tough situation and you handled it better than I ever hoped you could."

Nathan was squirming now, and he finally slipped off the couch. Then he walked over to Kim and looked up at her. Kim picked him up and pulled him onto her lap. He settled in against her, as though he liked her very much.

"That's amazing," the coach said. "He usually doesn't warm up to people that way—not so quickly anyway."

Kim liked that, but it was only making her situation more awkward. She was trying to sort all this out in her mind. And now she had a new worry. "So...do you feel I'm letting everyone down if I quit?"

"I'm sorry, Kim, but yes, I do. You tried out. You made the team. And now, just when we're about to start our regular season matches, you want to walk away from it. That's definitely going to hurt us. I'll try to pick up another player from the recreational league. But there's no one out there who can do as much for us."

Kim nodded. And she thought some more. She

had never been a quitter. She had never let her team down before. She didn't want to do that. "Well, maybe I'll keep trying then," she said.

"That's good news, Kim. But I don't want you to do it unless you can give the game everything you have. And you have to know you'll be a substitute. If you can't stand spending a lot of time on the sidelines, you might as well quit right now."

"No. I can handle that part. But what if I decide later that soccer is hurting my softball, and I'm not getting that good at soccer?"

"That's up to you, Kim. But if you're going to stay, I want you to stay with us all season."

"Well…all right." Kim got up. She set Nathan down and then knelt and said good-bye to him. He wouldn't speak, but he smiled at her.

The coach gave Kim a little pat on the back and thanked her. "Don't worry about Allie," she said. "She talks before she thinks sometimes. The main thing is, I think you know within yourself that you're doing the right thing."

"Yeah. I guess I am."

But as Kim walked out the door, she was already wondering. She was glad she hadn't said anything to Dawn or to her parents, but now she had to tell Kelsie. More than that, she had to go home, get her stuff, and then show up for practice. And that meant facing Allie and all the others.

Kim knew that she didn't have to be the star of

the team to be satisfied, but she also knew she would never be really happy until she could offer more to the team than she was offering right now. An angry little part of her kept saying, "You can be as good as Allie by the end of the season if you give it everything you have." Maybe that was a part of her that the coach didn't understand.

At practice that night, Kim worked very hard. And she looked pretty good at times. In fact, during defensive drills, she looked strong. But her attack skills were weak, and she knew it. She was still not accurate with her passes, and she felt really uncoordinated sometimes when she had to control a ball that was flying through the air at her.

Allie didn't say anything more about the last match. No one did, really. But once, after Kim had tried a shot and had gotten under the ball too much and lifted it way over the goal, she glanced over at Allie. And Allie was laughing.

Kim told herself that she was going to practice more—on her own, the way Dawn always did. Maybe tomorrow night she and Dawn could get together and...but tomorrow night was softball practice.

Kim really did feel she had done the right thing, considering the whole situation. But she wished she had never gone out for soccer in the first place.

41

That night, Kelsie didn't help much. She told Kim, "Well, it's your decision. I won't say anything more about it." But Kim heard the ice in her voice.

If things were complicated at that point, they got a lot more so at the next soccer match—the first league match.

When the match started, Kim was on the side-lines, watching. No matter what she had told the coach—and herself—being a backup player was still not easy for her.

The opponents were the Plano Wildcats, and Kim knew some of the girls from competing against them in other sports. The Wildcats had a middle forward named Leslie Hermann, who was good at anything she played. They also had a midfielder named Cindy Ngu, who was quick and very skilled with the ball.

The match had hardly gotten started before Cindy broke past Lorrie and made a run at the goal. She slammed a hard shot that was only a foot or so wide. The Striders on the sidelines all took a sigh of relief. But only a minute or so later, on a corner kick, Leslie leaped high, timed her jump perfectly, and banged a header into the net.

Coach Diaz was upset with her defense for not blocking out better. And the girls on the side of the field were saying, "We can't give this team easy goals. They're too good."

For the first time, the thought began to creep into Kim's mind that she was better off on the sidelines.

That's when everything suddenly changed. The ball got knocked around in the middle of the field for a while, but then a Wildcat wing made a long pass downfield. Pam, the sweeper, ran to the ball and reached for it with her leg extended. Just then a Wildcat midfielder came charging in, also trying to get to the ball. The midfielder kicked hard, and the two legs met.

Both girls went down. And both stayed down.

After the whistle sounded and play stopped, the Wildcat player slowly got up. But Pam didn't. She was lying on her side, with her right leg pulled up in front of her and her hands clutching her shin.

The coach ran out—and everyone waited. Pam got up, but it was clear that she couldn't walk without help. A couple of the players bent low, got under her arms, and then helped her to the sidelines.

Coach Diaz walked with the girls until they neared the touchline. Then she turned and said, "Kim, you're going in. You may have to play a lot today."

Kim felt a flight of butterflies take off in her stomach.

# CHAPTER 6

Kim ran onto the field and checked in with the referee. Shawndra Cooper received the throw-in and then blasted a long pass toward midfield. Kim was happy to see the play move in the other direction. As the sweeper, she was the last stopper before the goalie, once the ball got close to her own goal. She ran up the field a little way, but she knew she couldn't let Leslie get away from her.

The Striders seemed to be pushing a little harder now—maybe because they were behind by a goal, or maybe because they knew they would have to make up for losing Pam. Dawn made a good pass to Rachel, who was to the right of the goal area, but a defender marked her close and she couldn't get a shot off.

When Rachel tried a centering pass, a Wildcat fullback got to the ball and banged it up the field.

Allie went after the ball, but the Wildcats' Cindy Ngu was too quick for her. Cindy controlled the ball, dribbled a few yards, and then booted a pass toward her teammate Leslie.

But Kim was there. She fought Leslie for the ball and managed to kick it away. Marsella knocked the ball back upfield, and the Strider attack took over again.

Kim felt relieved. She wasn't sure she could make a whole lot happen on attack, but she at least didn't want to be the one to make a mistake and give up a cheap score.

The battle stayed tough in the middle of the field for a while. Both teams were running very hard, and neither could seem to mount much of an attack. Kim stayed back maybe a little more than she had to, but she didn't want to get caught out of position.

Then a Wildcat midfielder got the ball outside to a wing, and the wing broke down the touchline on a good run. Shawndra was keeping her outside, however, and Kim was all over Leslie. The Striders got back quickly, and the threat didn't look that serious.

Suddenly, however, the wing pulled up and shook loose from Shawndra. The wing was open long enough to blast a high pass toward the goal area.

Kim thought of going for the ball, but when she

saw that Leslie had the angle on her, she played it safe. She tucked in behind as Leslie controlled the ball against her body and then let it drop to the grass.

Kim was ready. She and Leslie were directly in front of the goal, maybe thirty feet away.

With her back to Kim, Leslie faked right and then cut left. Kim reacted well and stayed with her. She even reached in and deflected the ball, but Leslie was able to run after it and save it before anyone else could get to it.

Leslie faced Kim now and tried another break, back to her left. Kim reacted well again, staying in a good position. But she couldn't get close enough to go for a steal.

Kim was expecting something tricky now, but instead Leslie spotted the other middle forward breaking toward her. She dropped a pass away from the goal area toward her teammate.

And that's when Lorrie made a mistake. She rushed in and tried to steal the ball, but she reached out too far, which left her off balance. The forward was able to push the ball past her and break toward the goal.

For an instant, Kim thought of cutting over to take on the forward, but she knew that Leslie would then be left wide open. So Kim stayed with Leslie, hoping that someone would pick up the other girl.

But no one was there. Franny came out of the goal and rushed at the forward, but the forward pulled up and lifted a little looping shot that dropped behind Franny.

Franny tried to stop and get back, but it was too late. The ball arched over her head and rolled into the net. The score was suddenly 2 to 0, and the Striders were in trouble.

Kim felt bad. But at least, she told herself, the goal wasn't her fault this time. Lorrie had made the mistake.

The Wildcats seemed to take the goal in stride. They celebrated a little, but they didn't go crazy. Kim had the feeling that they were starting to think the match wasn't going to be that tough.

More than anything, Kim wished she was good enough to play forward, to make a fantastic move and blast a shot home. That's what she had always done in other sports. She had made things happen.

The battle, however, moved back to the middle of the field. The Striders were working very hard, but they couldn't seem to get open for a reasonable shot.

Then they got a break.

As halftime was coming up, a Wildcat fullback made a sloppy pass to the outside. Heather ran in and controlled the ball. When she saw Dawn running toward her, Heather kicked the ball over to her.

Dawn was open for a moment and tried to make

a run to the goal, but the defense closed quickly. So she tried a long shot that seemed to have no chance.

The ball was rolling toward the goalie, who was ready to scoop it up. But she slipped just as she was reaching for the ball. It bounced off her shoulder and rolled back toward the front of the goal area.

Crystal happened to be in just the right spot. She dashed to the ball, beating her defender by a step, and fired it low and hard at the goal. The goalie had recovered by now. She reached for the ball, but she was an instant late, and the ball caught the net.

The score was 2 to 1. The Striders were back in the game!

And the girls didn't mind showing that they were happy. They all ran to Crystal. Those who could get close enough grabbed hold of her, and the others reached over shoulders to give her a slap.

Kim felt some of the pressure release. There was lots of time left, and the Striders could score a couple more. They just had to keep the Wildcats from scoring again themselves.

That's exactly what Coach Diaz told the team at halftime. She let the girls get a drink of water, and then she asked them to sit down on the grass, near the side of the field. "Girls," she said, "you got a break, and you're still in this game. But you're going to have to play a lot better in the second half to have any chance of winning."

Dawn was sitting next to Kim. "We can do it, too," she whispered. "We beat this team easily last year."

Kim wondered, could she be the difference? But she told herself no. She hadn't really messed up. Pam couldn't have done any better.

"Allie and Anne," the coach said, "when you get the chance, double on Cindy Ngu. The other midfielder isn't that much of a threat to us. We need to stop Cindy from controlling the middle of the field."

Kim was nodding. It was something she had done plenty in basketball—take away the offense by shutting down the other team's best player.

"Crystal and Dawn, you can't wait for passes all the time. You have to get in the middle of things and get that ball. We're spending most of our time on defense, and we can't catch this team that way."

That made sense to Kim, too. In softball, sometimes you had to take a chance to make something happen. Go for the extra base on a hit, or steal third—whatever it took. You had to fire up your team.

"And fullbacks, you've stayed pretty tough, considering all the pressure they've had on you. A couple of mistakes, though, and that's the difference in this game."

The coach was looking at Kim, not at Lorrie. Kim was shocked.

"Kim, you don't have the experience to know this, but when you get caught between two attackers, you have to stop the one with the ball. If you let someone go straight to the goal, you know you're in big trouble. But if you force her to pass, she might make a bad pass and buy you some time to get help from someone else."

Kim nodded, but a sick feeling struck her stomach. She was thinking of a two-on-one fastbreak in basketball. The defender was always supposed to key on the player with the ball, and force her to make a pass. She was never supposed to let the dribbler go straight to the hoop for a layup. Kim *knew* that. It was what she had always been taught.

She knew something else besides. She had played it safe. She had been worried more about Leslie—*her* mark—scoring than she had been about stopping the goal.

"But listen, girls, you didn't play bad defense. The problem is, you played *too much* defense. We need to get the ball and go with it. Get some pressure on *their* defense. And that means every one of you has to be part of the attack. If you fullbacks think of yourselves only as defenders, we're not going at them with enough power."

Lorrie asked the question that was on Kim's

mind. "But if we get caught in the middle of the field, and someone breaks away, you'll be upset with us."

"No. Not necessarily. Someone has to stay back, but it isn't always the fullbacks. If you can take the ball forward, do it—and you midfielders, if you see that happening, drop back in their places. That's how the powerful soccer teams play it. That's called 'total soccer.'"

Kim was thinking things over. She had made a mistake after all, and she had given up a goal. Besides that, she had stayed back too much, and that was one of the reasons the attack wasn't going well. It all came down to the same thing again. She was hurting her team.

But she wasn't going to back away. She had to do something about it in the second half.

Now the coach was looking at her again. "Pam bruised her leg pretty badly, Kim. She might even have a broken bone. Her parents took her to the emergency room. I don't think she'll be playing for a while. You're going to get thrown into the middle of things—and not just for today. But don't worry, you can handle it."

That's what Kim wanted to believe. She told herself this was it. She had to step in now and do something big.

# CHAPTER

# 7

Kim knew what she had to do when she walked onto the field. She had to get involved in the attack. She still had to think defense, but she also had to use her speed and make something happen farther up the field.

In a way, the idea was exciting. No more playing scared. She would think about soccer the way she had always thought about other sports. She wasn't going to sit back and worry about making mistakes. She was going to do something positive.

It didn't take long before her new attitude made a difference. She saw a wing glance toward Leslie, and she knew a pass was coming—just the way she knew it on the basketball court. She cut inside Leslie and stole the pass, and then she knocked the ball toward Anne, who was moving upfield.

Then Kim ran with Anne. She kept her eye on

Leslie, but she moved farther up than usual. When a Wildcat player deflected a pass and the ball rolled free, she used her speed to get to it and then bang it toward Heather on the side of the field.

Heather took the ball along the touchline and then tried to pass back toward the center to Allie. Allie got cut off and couldn't get to the ball, but Dawn had worked her way into the middle of the field. When the Wildcat midfielder tried to dribble, Dawn stepped in and stole the ball back. Then Dawn made a good lead pass to Rachel, who was cutting on an angle toward the goal.

But the whistle sounded.

Rachel had gotten a little too far ahead, and the referee called her for being offside. But at least the Strider attack had looked a lot stronger.

"That's better out there," Coach Diaz was shouting.

A couple of minutes later, the attack was moving again. Kim was forcing Leslie to work on defense now, and that was keeping Leslie from doubling on other girls.

But it was Dawn who made a great move. She stepped in and tackled a Wildcat midfielder. She took control of the ball and booted it over to Allie. Then she cut right past Allie and took a return pass.

Dawn ran hard with the ball until she attracted

two defenders. Then she cut off her run and dropped the ball back to Heather.

Dawn didn't stop working. She ran with Heather and then angled away, toward the goal. Heather pulled up, but she was well defended. She tried to get the ball to Crystal since she had no angle to make the pass to Dawn.

Crystal and a Wildcat fullback fought for the ball, and the ball got knocked loose. But Dawn had made a move back to Crystal and was there to receive the pass.

Dawn broke toward the goal, slowed, and then broke again. And she got past her defender.

She was coming from the right side, and the goalie took the right corner away from her. But Dawn drove the ball across the goal to the left.

The goalie dove for the ball, but it got by her and sliced just inside the left goalpost.

Goal!

The score was tied, 2 to 2. And the Striders had turned into believers.

They didn't celebrate as wildly this time, however. Everyone was sounding intent and determined. "Let's get another one!" they were all yelling.

Kim lined up and waited for the kickoff. She knew now that she was becoming part of this team. She hadn't done anything spectacular, but she had held her own on defense, and she had gotten into the attack.

But the Wildcats came back furiously this time. If they had been a little overconfident before, they weren't now.

Leslie was running especially hard. Kim knew that she was getting frustrated. Once, when the action broke for a moment, Leslie leaned over to catch her breath. Then she said, "I'm going to score on you. You're not a soccer player."

Kim didn't like that kind of stuff. During a game, she would say "Good shot" or "Nice play," but she never talked tough, never bragged. And she didn't think much of players who did. So she said nothing, but she told herself that Leslie wasn't going to score on her, no matter what. She played the girl tighter than ever.

Time was getting away, however, and both teams were pressing. Kim wanted to do something more, something that could fire the attack.

And so, when the Striders got control of the ball, she moved up fast. When she took a pass on the side of the field, she used her speed to beat her defender and make a break. She ran as fast as she could, and she tried to keep the ball under control. But she wasn't much of a dribbler, and the ball got away from her. It rolled across the touchline, out of bounds.

She wasn't satisfied. She was going to get the ball back. She marked Leslie and waited for the throw-in. But she gave Leslie a little room, hoping that she could anticipate the pass and make a steal.

Sure enough, the throw arched toward Leslie, and Kim made her move. She broke in front and jumped high to knock the ball away with her head. But she jumped just an instant too late, and the ball got over her.

Leslie took the pass and broke upfield, going hard—all alone.

A breakaway.

Kim landed off balance and stumbled. She caught herself quickly, however, and took off. She ran all out, and she gradually made up the ground on Leslie.

But too late.

Just as Kim caught up, Leslie took the shot. Franny had charged her and seemed to be in a good position. But Leslie hit a cannon shot directly past Franny's feet.

And into the goal.

The score was 3 to 2. Kim couldn't believe it.

Leslie spun around and pointed a finger at Kim. "I told you," she shouted. "You've got a lot to learn about this game."

Kim turned and walked away.

Now another girl was running onto the field. "I'm in for you, Kim," she said. It was one of the substitutes, a girl named Amber Bristol.

Kim walked slowly off the field. When she got

to the sideline, the coach was waiting. "It's okay, Kim. I left you in too long because you were doing so well. But you've got to be tired by now. That's the only reason I'm taking you out."

"I messed up," Kim said.

"Of course you did. That's going to happen sometimes. Every time someone scores, someone has messed up. That's soccer. But you did some real growing today. You're learning fast."

She was learning all right, Kim told herself. At the expense of the team.

Things only got worse after that. Marsella got faked on a good move by a Wildcat wing, and the wing made a perfect crossing pass. Leslie leaped high and slammed a header into the goal.

And that was it.

The Striders worked hard, but they couldn't manage another score. They lost, 4 to 2.

The Striders had won the championship the year before, and most of the best players were still on the team. But now they were walking off the field with their heads down, wondering when they would get their first win.

The coach, however, wasn't about to let them act that way. "Hey, kids, you played well. I saw some great things happening out there. We have some weaknesses we have to work on. But we get to play these Wildcats again before the year is over. And we're going to beat them next time. In fact, I still think we're going to win the championship."

She got very little reaction, so she said, "Do you believe that?"

"Yeah!" they shouted. But Kim didn't feel any real conviction inside herself—or in any of the girls around her.

The real surprise came when Dawn—supposedly her best friend—turned to her and said, "I hope Pam will be back soon. We need her."

"Thanks a lot," Kim said, and she spun to walk away.

Dawn grabbed her arm and pulled her back. "Kim, that's nothing against you. You played great today. But we need Pam, too. She's one of our best players."

Kim tried to calm down. She didn't want to act like a little kid. She took a long breath, and then she said, "Dawn, tell me the truth. Would we have won if Pam hadn't got hurt?"

"It's hard to say, Kim. It might not have made that much difference. We gave up that first goal before she got hurt."

"But she wouldn't have gone for that throw-in and let Leslie get away the way I did."

"Maybe not. But, Kim, your idea was right. If you had stolen the ball and we had ended up scoring, everyone would be saying what a great move it was."

58

"What are they saying now?"

"Nothing. I haven't heard anyone say one thing. We just didn't play well enough to win."

"Allie is probably saying plenty—or at least thinking it."

"Kim, that's her problem. You can't worry about that. You improved a hundred percent over last game. You got involved in the attack, you stole the ball—and most of the time, you stopped Leslie. That's not easy to do."

Kim nodded, and she pretended to accept that. But she turned away and then whispered, "I blew it again."

# CHAPTER 8

When Kim got home, she was still feeling rotten, but she didn't want to get into another conversation with her dad. So she only told her parents the Striders had lost. She tried not to show much emotion, and she didn't give a lot of details.

She hadn't been home long, however, before Kelsie called. "I heard what happened at your game," she said.

"Yeah. We lost."

"Well, I know. But I heard that Pam got hurt and you had to play way too much."

"Too much? What's that supposed to mean?"

"More than you're really ready to play, I guess."

"Who told you that?"

Kim heard nothing but silence for a time. Finally, Kelsie said, "That's just what someone said."

"Who, Kelsie? Come on, tell me."

"Well…it was actually one of the softball players. She had talked to some girls on the soccer team. I don't think they meant it as an insult or anything. They didn't say you played so bad. They just said you weren't ready to take over for Pam yet. I think they sort of felt sorry for you."

Kim didn't know whether she was angry or hurt. She couldn't think what to say to Kelsie.

"Kim, don't take it like that. Dawn told me that you're picking up the game so fast you're going to be great at it. You just haven't had enough experience."

"Do you know which girls said it, Kelsie? Was Allie one of them?"

"Maybe. I really don't know."

"Look…I've got to go."

"Kim, I'm sorry I said anything. But maybe you should think about…well, never mind."

"What?"

"Well, I guess I shouldn't bring this all up again. But I still think you would have more fun—and do better—if you just let this whole soccer thing drop."

Kim was lying back on her bed. "Maybe I should have done that last week—when I had my mind made up. But now that Pam's hurt, I really can't."

"I heard Pam's not hurt that bad. She'll probably only miss one game, maybe two."

Kim stared at the ceiling. "Well, we'll see. I don't know. I'll see you at school tomorrow."

She hung up the phone. But then she picked it back up immediately. She called Dawn and told her what Kelsie had said.

"Oh come on, Kim," Dawn said, sounding angry. "Kelsie just wants you to quit playing soccer. She's trying to stir up trouble."

"I don't think so," Kim said. "She knew Pam got hurt and that I had had to play a lot. And I guess, according to the girls on our team, I didn't do a good enough job."

"Okay, Kim. I'll say it: You aren't as good as Pam yet. Is that so surprising?"

"No. I'm not saying that. I know I have a lot to learn. I just don't see why our team has to go around talking behind my back—saying I lost the game. I did the best I could."

"I told you already. It wasn't your fault. And I don't think any girl on our team said that it was. I just think Kelsie made it sound that way to get you mad at us."

"Oh, man." Kim let her breath blow out. "I wish I had *never* let you talk me into playing soccer."

"Kim, think about it. What are you really saying?"

"What do you mean?"

"When we were younger, and we played basketball together, you were out there making all the baskets and I was sitting on the bench. I know what it's like to do my very best and not be very good. Now, for the first time, you're not the best player on the team, and you're telling me you can't take that."

"That's not true," said Kim. "I just don't want my teammates saying I lost the game."

"If someone put the blame on you for losing the match, that was wrong. But I don't think that's what's really bothering you. You just thought you could play soccer for a few weeks and be as good as anyone—or better."

"Dawn, I can't believe you're saying that. You sound just like Allie. I decided to play only because you talked me into it. And now I wish I hadn't."

"I wish you hadn't either, Kim. I had no idea you would act like this."

"Well, fine. Now I *am* going to quit. See you around."

She slammed the phone down. Then she sat up. She was mad enough to hit something, but she didn't know what to hit—or what to do.

She didn't want to talk to her parents about this, not after what her dad had said before. She thought of calling Kelsie back, to tell her she was going to be a full-time softball player again. Something about that didn't feel right, either.

But why not? What was wrong with her? She just couldn't sort out what she was feeling right now.

She sat on the edge of her bed and looked straight ahead, trying to think why she had reacted so strongly. She could see herself in the mirror over her chest of drawers. What she expected to see was anger in her eyes, but she saw confusion.

After another minute or so, she lay back on the bed again, grabbed a pillow, and stuffed her face into it. She didn't want to admit what she was beginning to feel.

After about fifteen minutes, however, and a lot of calming down, some things were beginning to come clear to her—things she had a hard time admitting to herself. It wasn't easy, but she picked up the phone and called Dawn back.

"Dawn, I'm sorry," she said.

"That's okay. I'm sorry, too. I shouldn't have said some of that stuff."

"No. I think…you're partly right about me. I told myself I wouldn't be very good at soccer. But maybe I never really believed it."

"I keep telling you, you're doing fine, Kim."

"Yeah. Sort of. But it seemed like if I could run fast, and had good coordination, it wouldn't take long to learn the passing and shooting and stuff. It's harder than it looks."

"Yup. That's true."

"I can accept the idea that I have a lot to learn. I

just can't handle the idea that a team would lose because I'm playing."

"So are you quitting?"

"I wish I could. That's what I *want* to do. I don't think I ever should have started. But I've got to stay on at least until Pam gets back. The girls would have a right to hate me if I quit right now."

"Kim, let's work out together. Let's get together every night, if we have to, and I'll help you with your dribbling and passing."

"How can I do that? I have softball games on Saturdays and practice on Wednesdays. And the team gets together a lot of other nights. And the players are always telling me I need to be there more."

"Kim, you don't need that much practice in softball."

"I'm not hitting well, Dawn. My timing is all off this year. I need to take more batting practice."

"You'll hit, Kim. You always have. That's because you started playing softball when you were eight years old. But you need to work to catch up with your soccer skills."

"I don't know."

"Think about it. You started all the other sports when you were really young, and you were the best, right from the beginning. You were learning all the time, but you weren't catching up. This is the first time you've had a real challenge, Kim. The other sports have all been easy for you."

"No matter how hard I work this year, I'll never make the starting team."

"So what? Every team has substitutes. You've just never been one before. Can't you be the star of the *second* team?"

It was a surprising idea—one that Kim had never thought of. She had always felt sorry for the girls who sat on the bench and waited for a chance to play. She had never realized what they offered a team.

But something about it sounded right. "Maybe I can think about it that way," she finally said. "I'll try to find as much time as I can. Maybe we can start working out tomorrow after school. I might have to work out with you for an hour or two and then run over to the softball diamond for a little while. But I guess I can do both."

And that's what Kim began to do. Almost every night she and Dawn worked out for at least half an hour. Dawn kept stressing the fundamentals, showing Kim how to drive her foot through the ball, how to lift it or to scoot it across the grass. And she worked on the short little taps with the inside of the foot that keep the ball under control while dribbling.

Kim did pick up athletic skills easily, but soccer

skills were entirely different from those of any other sport she had played. She found herself frustrated when the ball wouldn't do what she wanted it to do.

But she kept working. And she seemed to do better every night.

One other thing happened that took a little pressure off Kim. When she played her first softball game, her hitting wasn't so far off as she had feared. Something about the competition, and maybe knowing she was back on her own turf, brought the best out of her. She went 3 for 4 and drove in 3 runs. And she played shortstop like a wizard, scooping up ground balls and throwing arrows to first base. The team won easily, 9 to 2.

After the game, her teammates all told her how well she had played. Jamie Kaapu, the catcher, told her, "Great game!" But then she said, "Kim, you ought to stick with softball. That's your sport."

Jamie didn't seem to intend any cheap shots, but Kim was a little annoyed. "Look," she said, pointing her finger at Jamie, "I made a promise to the soccer players, and I'm going to keep it. I can't quit now."

Kelsie was standing nearby. She laughed and said, "Hey, as long as you play the way you did today, you can play ten other sports at the same time."

Kim was embarrassed. She looked back at Jamie.

"I feel at home with this game. I love it. And I don't feel that way when I play soccer. But I have to keep my promise."

"We know that," Kelsie said. "I'm *never* going to bring that up again." She laughed. "Unless you don't get a hit in the next game."

"Sure, Kelsie. At least my head was in the game the whole time. I saw what *you* were looking at every time you got a chance—all those guys from the boys' baseball team who were sitting in the bleachers."

"Kim, that's a big lie."

"No way. I saw you gawking over there every time—"

"Maybe so. But I wasn't looking at *all* of them. Only one."

"Which one?"

"Never mind. Besides, the guys weren't looking back at me. They were all watching you."

"No way," Kim said, but the truth was, she had noticed some of the guys looking.

More important, the tension between Kelsie and her seemed to be gone now. And that made everything better.

# CHAPTER 9

The next soccer match was Kim's real worry. Pam was there—but only to watch from the sidelines. Kim would be starting. It's what she had wanted at one time, but now she was not really comfortable with that much responsibility.

The opposing team was called the Roadrunners. They hadn't been all that good the year before, but they had won their first match this year, and everyone was saying that they had improved a great deal. A new midfielder from Argentina named Juanita Tangona seemed to be the big difference. She wasn't so much a shooter and scorer as she was a dominating power in the middle.

As the match got started, Kim soon saw what Juanita could do. She had dazzling footwork. The ball seemed under some magic power when she moved with it—like a trained pet that obeyed her commands. It was a pretty thing to watch, but terrifying when she came into Kim's part of the field.

Kim was marking a forward most of the time—a big, strong girl named Nicki Silva. Kim had played against her in basketball, and she had an idea of what to expect. Nicki wasn't fancy. She wasn't even all that quick. But she never quit working, and she used her size to advantage when she got the chance.

Kim had learned the hard way that playing an almost flawless game wasn't always enough. One or two mistakes, close to the goal, could turn a whole match around.

That's what soccer came down to—lots of work, lots of running, lots of great moves. But not many goals. So a defender had to be consistent and ready, and tough as nails once the ball got within shooting range.

The early part of the match was intense for the Strider defense. Juanita was all over the middle of the field, keeping the pressure on the attack for the Roadrunners. That meant the ball kept moving toward Kim, and she had to work hard almost all the time.

Nicki, Kim's mark, never stopped moving, trying to slip away for a pass. After the first five minutes of shadowing her, Kim was breathing hard and hoping the Striders would take the ball the other way so that the fullbacks could get a little rest.

But when the Striders did get a drive going, and

Kim slowed to a walk as the action moved away from her, she heard Coach Diaz yell, "Get on the attack, Kim. Make something happen."

Kim trotted forward, panting for air and wondering how she would make it through a whole match this way.

What the Striders soon learned, however, was that a couple of the Roadrunners were really not very skilled. The defenders began to see that they could drop off these weaker players and double-team Juanita. Once they began to do that, the Roadrunners' attack began to slow down.

Kim was still running hard to stay with Nicki, but at least the ball wasn't coming straight at her as often as it had in the first few minutes.

The problem was, no one had scored, and Kim knew the coach was right. She had to play more of a role on the attack.

Halfway through the first half, the score was still 0 to 0 when Anne moved over to help Allie double-team Juanita. Juanita tried to slip between them, but Anne got her foot on the ball.

Anne couldn't control the ball, but that turned out not to be a problem. The Roadrunners made a bad pass and knocked the ball out of bounds.

As the teams got ready for the throw-in, Kim jogged farther up the field than usual. Anne tossed a short pass to Marsella, and Marsella hit the ball over to Allie, who dribbled forward. She looked

71

downfield and watched for an opportunity. When Allie's defender moved in tight, Kim suddenly broke forward, taking her defender by surprise.

Allie saw that Kim was open and scooted a little pass in front of her. Kim dribbled the ball a few yards but didn't try to run too far. She slowed, spotted Heather along the left touchline, and drove a pass in her direction. Her hard work all week had paid off. She put a nice loft on the ball and dropped it close to Heather, who was able to break quickly up the field and then shoot a pass toward Crystal.

Kim checked to see where Nicki was. She didn't want to get caught too far into the middle of things and not be able to get back on defense.

Heather's looping pass to Crystal attracted a crowd. Two of the Roadrunner fullbacks sandwiched Crystal, and one of them got her head on the ball and drove it away from the goal.

The ball bounded up the center of the field, and Kim saw her chance. She turned on her speed, darted to the ball, and then rocketed a hard pass directly back to Crystal.

The same two fullbacks tried to stop the pass again, and some shoulders banged. But Crystal took the ball on the volley, hit it with the inside of her foot, and knocked it over to Dawn.

Dawn was well marked, but she saw Crystal spin and break between her two defenders. Heather was also cutting in from the outside, and she was all alone.

Dawn hit a low pass that was a little short. Crystal had to stop and fight for the ball as her defenders caught up with her. But she managed to punch it out toward Heather.

And Heather had a shot. She powered the ball at the goal.

The goalie had gotten herself into a perfect position, however. The shot came in high, and the goalie got her hands up and blocked it. But she couldn't hang on to the ball, and it rolled back toward Heather. Heather blasted another shot, and Kim, watching from some distance away, thought it might go in this time.

But the goal area was crowded now, and the ball bounced off a fullback's ankles and rolled away. Kim saw a Roadrunner take control of the ball and look upfield.

Kim started backpedaling, fast, and she watched to see what Nicki would do.

Then she heard a shout. She looked back toward the goal. Dawn and Crystal had grabbed each other and were jumping up and down.

The ball was in the net.

Kim took off toward the goal to celebrate, but she still didn't know how the ball had gotten in.

"I was looking the other way. Who got the goal?" Kim shouted above the noise.

Dawn was beaming. "I did. That fullback got the ball, but Crystal stole it and passed it back to me. I just turned and slammed it in."

"That's great! That's great!" Kim shouted. "Let's keep it up."

"Kim, you were great. You ran for the ball, and you passed it down here. After that, we got lucky, really. But if we don't get the ball to this end of the field, we can't score. And you're the one who got it here."

Kim grinned. She liked that. She would like to bang one home herself sometime, just to see what it was like. But she was starting to see how much of a team sport soccer really was.

In most sports a player could do something on her own—hit a home run, shoot a three-point basket, spike a ball over the net—but in soccer, everyone had to work just to get the ball into shooting range. Even a girl who didn't get near the ball had to be running and trying to get open, pulling a defender with her.

Kim jogged back to her position. She wanted some more of this. The score was 1 to 0 now, but the Striders could use another goal before halftime. They also needed to stay tough on defense and not give up this lead.

The problem was that the Roadrunners were psyched up now. They didn't want to get any further behind. They came hard on the attack.

Juanita was being cut off most of the time now, but she was drawing two defenders to her. That could always create some danger.

Finally one of those "weak" players, left open, hit a long pass straight down the middle of the field, toward the goal area. Kim was tempted to break to the ball, but she wasn't sure she could get there in time. She didn't dare leave Nicki open, so she stayed with her.

Lorrie and a Roadrunner forward got to the ball about the same time, and neither could control it. They jumped and knocked each other out of the way. Both came down off balance, and the ball hit Lorrie's foot and glanced low and hard across the front of the goal area.

Nicki, who had a better angle to the ball than Kim did, dashed toward it. Kim got herself in a good defensive position, ready for anything. She waited to see what Nicki would do.

Nicki stopped the ball and then stepped over it and faced Kim. She faked left, but Kim kept her control, low, with her shoulders square to Nicki.

Nicki had wanted to break right, but Kim cut her off. Nicki pulled up, and in that instant Kim moved in. She used her shoulder to hold Nicki from driving around her, and she kicked at the ball. The ball glanced off both their legs and bounced away.

It was a scary moment. The ball was rolling free in the goal area. Someone had to get to it.

Franny broke from the goal just as Nicki pushed past Kim and ran for it. But Kim spun and made a quick move herself. She made up the step that Nicki had gotten on her.

Franny never would have made it in time. And she would have been badly out of position. But Kim was able to reach out and push the ball at Franny, just before Nicki could get to it.

Franny picked up the ball, ran to a clear spot, and then punted it away. The threat was over.

Kim wasn't sure she had handled everything exactly the way she should have. But she knew her quickness had made the difference. She had come through when she had to.

The next time the action stopped, Nicki gasped between breaths, "Hey, Kim, you're better than I expected. I thought you didn't know how to play this game."

"I'm trying to learn it," Kim said, also panting.

"I hate to think what you'll do once you get some experience. You're going to be tough."

When halftime came, and the score was still 1 to 0, Kim had those words to remember. But she also knew that the team had another half to go. Next time, Nicki might make a different move. One mistake and Kim would be right back where she had been the last two matches.

# CHAPTER 10

Coach Diaz had lots of good things to say to everyone, and she even singled Kim out. "You played tough out there, Kim," she said. "I've never seen a player work any harder on defense than you've been working. Every girl here could learn something from that. What you lack in experience, you're more than making up for with sheer effort."

That was not the sort of compliment Kim had gotten used to in her life. Right now, though, it sounded pretty good.

But then she was taken by surprise. "Kim, take a rest now for a little while. Amber is coming in for you."

Amber? The idea scared Kim. Amber had played a lot of soccer, and she had some good skills. But she was slow and sort of delicate. Kim had the feeling that Nicki would work her over. Why not put her in the middle of the field where she could play against one of those weak players?

Kim told herself the coach must know what she was doing. But as the second half got under way, she was worried.

And the first time Nicki got control of the ball, she forced her way right past Amber and got off a good shot. Franny made a great stop, so no harm was done, but Kim wondered if it wasn't just a matter of time until Nicki scored.

Kim wanted to get back on the field. Right now it seemed as though she would rather go out there and make a mistake again than stand on the sidelines and watch Amber blow everything they had accomplished.

Just then the coach stepped up next to Kim. "Did you see what Amber just did?"

"Yeah. She got run right over."

"Not really. She knows she's not very fast. And she can't muscle a big girl like Nicki. So she took Nicki's angle away. She stayed with her and forced her to the right of the goal. Nicki pushed through her, eventually, but by then Franny was in the right spot, and Nicki really didn't have anything to shoot at."

"Well...yeah...that makes sense." It was like forcing a girl to the baseline in basketball and leaving her no room to drive to the hoop.

"Amber doesn't have half your athletic ability,

and she'll never be a great player. But she's someone I can always depend on to go out there and play for part of a game and not hurt us."

Kim was no dummy. She didn't have to guess what the coach was trying to say to her. The coach needed good substitutes, and she wanted Kim to accept that same kind of role. But Kim had something else in mind. She was thinking how much she had been acting like Allie—expecting the worst from Amber.

"Nice job, Amber," she suddenly shouted. "Stay tough on Nicki."

The coach glanced toward her and smiled. Then she was striding off in the other direction, yelling to Anne to get tighter on Juanita.

Kim had never in her life wanted to be a cheerleader. She wasn't even one to make a lot of noise when she was playing in a game. She liked to lead the way by *doing*. But she found herself yelling now. The match was still one-zip, and the slightest little break in the defense could blow the lead.

But the break didn't come, and the battle was wearing down a lot of legs out on the field.

All through the match, Pam had been sitting on the grass in her street clothes. But now she got up and limped over to Kim. "It kills me to watch this," she said. "I'm not used to being over here."

"I know what you mean," Kim said, and the girls turned to watch the match.

Anne made a long lead pass toward Rachel on the wing. But a Roadrunner made a move to the ball first. She sent a pass back toward the middle of the field.

"How's your leg doing?" Kim asked.

"Not bad. I'll be back to practice next week."

Maybe Pam hadn't thought about it, but she was the one who was going to take away Kim's playing time. Kim didn't say that, though. She said, "That's good," and even though she had some mixed emotions, she knew she meant it.

Kim kept watching Amber. And she began to see how much the angles of the game counted on defense. An attacker could rarely score when the defenders gave her little of the goal to shoot at. It was true that a good defender marked a player closely. But running everywhere the attacker ran was wasted motion. The main thing was to keep the attacker from breaking inside and getting a clear path to the goal.

The defender also had to see the passing angles and force the attacker into positions that would take her out of a place where she could get a good pass. This really wasn't so different from basketball.

So Kim kept watching, trying to learn. And she also kept worrying.

But on and on the battle went, and no one scored. In fact, neither team was getting close enough to the goal even to shoot.

Then Kim heard her name. "Kim, Shawndra—let's get some fresh legs back out there. Go in for Amber and Marsella."

The next time the action stopped, Kim ran back onto the field. Now she hoped she could do as well as Amber had done. "Nice job. Great defense," she told Amber.

Nicki walked over to her and grinned. "I think I'm glad to have you back. That skinny little girl is tough to deal with."

"Yeah. I noticed that."

But the friendliness was all gone once Nicki got a chance to score. She cut away from Kim and took a pass. Then she spun and drove straight ahead.

Kim faced her and waited. But she sidestepped a little toward the middle of the field and forced Nicki to go outside. Then she ran with her and didn't try to do anything fancy—just keep her angling away from the goal.

The technique was perfect. Nicki was forced to take a poor shot that went behind the goalpost and over the end line.

Soon after that, the Striders made a good move upfield. Rachel ended up with the ball on the right side of the goal area. She tried to pass the ball to Dawn, but it was partially blocked.

Crystal ran the ball down. The defense packed in, and she couldn't get much of a shot off. The ball banged off a fullback, dangerously close to the Roadrunners' goal. But the goalie got to it and booted it out of her end of the field.

Kim had run hard to help with the attack. She was in a good spot to reach the ball first. She controlled the ball with her midsection—a trick that Dawn had been teaching her—and then she kicked a short pass to Anne.

Then some sort of instinct took over, and she knew what to do. It was called a give-and-go in basketball, a wall pass in soccer—the idea was to pass, break past the receiver, and receive a pass back, behind the defender.

And it worked to perfection. Kim took the pass and was wide open in the middle of the field. She hit the ball rather too far in front of her for good dribbling, but she ran it down and gave it another kick. Then she ran after it again.

When Heather came flying in on her left side, Kim was relieved to pass the ball off. She thought she'd better start dropping back quickly in case the Roadrunners took control of the ball.

But Heather got cut off. The defender got a foot on the ball, and it rolled loose.

Kim was closest to the ball again. She darted forward, farther up the field than she had ever been. She hoped a midfielder had dropped back to cover on defense.

She hit the ball forward, too long again, and for

a moment she thought a charging fullback would get to it. But Kim turned on that fifth gear of hers and *raced* to the ball. She seemed to surprise the defender with her speed. She hit the ball past the girl, slipped by, and chased the ball again.

Suddenly Kim realized that she was alone. A girl was running hard from the left, and another one was behind her. But there was nothing between her and the goal—except the goalie.

Kim gave the ball one more shove and ran after it again. Then, with the defender coming hard from the left, she knew she had to take her shot.

She didn't remember anything Dawn and the coach had told her. She just fired. But somehow she got it about right. She landed on her left foot and drove her right instep through the ball, with her weight forward and her arms wide and balanced.

She didn't hit the ball as low as she wanted to—not even as hard as she wanted to. But her line was perfect.

The ball sailed to the right side of the goal, just out of the reach of the goalie. And it went in.

It went in!

Kim couldn't have been more surprised if the skies had opened up and a brass band had come marching out of the clouds.

She had scored a goal!

A *big* goal!

The next thing she knew, dozens of girls—or so it seemed—had jumped on top of her. And more were landing all the time. She was down on the bottom, taking all this pounding, but she had never been so happy in her life.

Once she had hit a grand-slam homer in a league championship game. But she hadn't been *this* happy.

The celebration had to end, and Kim had to get up and go back to reality. But she played the rest of the game thinking all defense and not believing that any of this had really happened.

When it was all over, and the Striders had won, 2 to 0, the coach gave Kim a big hug. "Are you still thinking about quitting?" she asked.

"Yeah. I'm thinking about quitting softball," she said.


That night, Kim and Dawn talked for a long time. "Kim, you're going to end up a starter," Dawn told her.

"No. I doubt it. I still have a lot to learn," Kim said. But she wondered. Maybe she could crack the starting lineup, in time.

"If you keep playing, you'll end up a forward. Wouldn't it be great, if we could start together on the high school team?"

But that was a little too much to imagine. "Hold

84

on," Kim said. "Today is the first day I've even liked this game."

"The first day of many," Dawn said, grinning.

Kim had the feeling Dawn might be right. Later that night, she even admitted to her parents that scoring a goal in soccer was about as good as it gets.

Her dad was watching the late news, and he hadn't seemed to be paying much attention. But he turned to Kim and said, "Honey, this is bad news." He was grinning.

"Why?"

"You're just going to be a star at one more sport. I thought this game was going to teach you a few things."

"Don't worry, Dad," Kim said. "I'm no star. I'm just glad I'm not hurting the team as much as I was."

But when she went to bed that night, she remembered what Dawn had said. Starting on the soccer team might be a lot of fun—especially at forward. Maybe more fun than softball.

# CHAPTER 11

All the next week, Kim worked very hard. She and Dawn got together almost every day, and sometimes some of the other girls joined them. On the day of the official practice, Kim could see that Pam wasn't quite back to full speed. She was still favoring her injured leg, and she looked a little off on her timing.

Kim was almost sure she knew what that would mean.

So on the day of the match, Kim was excited. She was feeling a lot better about her attack skills, and she wanted to have a really good game. She was already thinking about the things Dawn had said. It would be great to play forward someday— or at least midfield, where she would get more chances to score. It was even tempting to think about taking Allie's position away from her, but she told herself not to think that way.

Then the coach announced the starting lineup. Pam was playing. Kim was on the sidelines.

Kim tried not to show any reaction, but she was shocked. She walked toward the touchline and stood by herself. She knew she ought to yell a little encouragement to her teammates, but she didn't have the heart.

No one knew what to expect from this team— the Hurricanes. A lot of the girls were new this year. But they had lost a close match the first week and had beaten a pretty good team the next week, so Coach Diaz was thinking that the team had to be pretty strong this year.

"What I hear," Coach Diaz told the girls before the match, "is that they're a sort of no-name team—no stars, no hot shots—but they work very well together."

The truth was that right now Kim wasn't thinking much about any of that. She was thinking a lot more about being pushed back to the sidelines. Did the coach really think Pam could play better, even with a bad leg? Hadn't Kim earned the right to be out there, the way she had played last time?

But soon after the kickoff, Kim saw something that took her by surprise. Pam was playing rugged defense, battling every second. Then a break in the action would come. As soon as she had the chance to rest, Pam would drop to one knee and massage her leg. And Kim could see she was in pain. When she walked, she couldn't avoid limping.

Each time, Kim would think, "She can't keep going. She's too tired. Her leg is hurting too much." But the action would start and Pam would play as hard as ever.

She was working well with the other fullbacks, too. They had all played together a long time, and they had a good sense of where the others would be. When the Hurricanes would get the ball into scoring territory, the midfielders would fall in with the fullbacks. Together, they would set up a solid pattern, each marking her own player, but switching off if they had to.

The coach had talked a lot about that. And Kim had learned to play match-up zones in basketball, but it was hard to do in soccer, where the players had more room to run.

Kim was starting to sense why she was on the sidelines.

The Strider defense was working perfectly, and the Hurricanes were not getting off shots that had much chance. But the problem was, the Hurricane defense was just as effective. Time and again, the Striders got the ball almost to a spot where one more pass, one opening, could mean a real chance to score. But the Hurricanes set up well, took attack angles away, and marked every player.

Finally, however, the Striders got control of the

ball near midfield, and Anne made a good pass to Rachel. Rachel tried to kick the ball toward the goal area, but a Hurricane forward blocked the pass, and the ball glanced away.

Allie ran to the ball and arrived at about the same time a Hurricane player did. Allie could have kicked at the ball, but instead she flicked her foot under it and popped it in the air toward herself. The Hurricane fullback lashed at the ball an instant late. Allie used the time when the fullback was still off balance to head the ball forward. Then she knifed past the defender and chased the ball down herself.

"Wow!" Kim screamed. "Great move, Allie! Take it to the goal!" Kim ran farther down the touchline to get a better look. She was amazed at what she had just seen.

Allie dribbled a few yards until another defender picked her up. She turned on the speed then, as though she were going to drive past on the right. But suddenly she pulled up and stopped the ball with the sole of her shoe. Then she lashed a crossing pass toward the goal area.

Dawn was there, but so was a defender. Dawn ran forward, knocked down the pass with the inside of her foot, and spun to take a shot.

The defender was charging hard. Dawn tried to slip a shot past her. But Kim, watching from a distance, saw it sail wide of the goal.

Until it curved!

The shot actually bent to the left. It was a looping shot, and the goalie was just as fooled by it as Kim had been. The goalie had cut to her left but had seen that the ball was going wide, and had let up.

But the ball hooked and dropped—just inside the goalpost and into the net.

The goalie dropped to her knees in frustration.

Dawn leaped in the air and did a full three-sixty, with her fist reaching for the sky.

Kim was running down the touchline, jumping and screaming. "How did she do that?" she kept yelling at no one in particular.

But it was the coach who eventually told her, "You can make a shot curve like that, if you know how to put the right spin on the ball. The trick is to know, in a split second, that that's the kind of shot you have to take—with the angle you have. And then you have to have the instinct to shoot it."

"Dawn knows what she's doing," Kim told the coach.

"Well, yeah. But it's natural with her now. She's been playing soccer for a long time, and she practices almost every day. That's the only way you get to be as good as Dawn is."

Kim knew that. She yelled at her teammates,

"Come on! Let's keep it going. Allie, that was a *great* move. Dawn, you're *awesome*."

But then she heard the coach. "Kim, I think we'd better give Pam a rest. Check in for her now."

Suddenly the idea was a little frightening to her again. She didn't want to let this team down. These girls deserved better than that. She was just starting to realize how good they were.

But Kim charged onto the field. And she soon got a tough test.

A Hurricane forward came at her hard, looking to get back that score and even things up. And maybe the forward thought she had a weaker defender in front of her now.

Kim shifted into the forward's path, and the girl pulled up. She turned and faked a pass—and Kim took the fake. She relaxed for just an instant.

The forward used the chance to push the ball past her on the right and then burst toward the goal.

Kim reacted quickly, spun and ran hard. She was pulling even with the forward just as the girl pulled back her leg and whipped a hard shot.

Kim somehow threw out her leg, skidding and then falling in the process. She didn't block the shot, but she got a piece of the ball just as the forward launched it. The pass flew higher than it might have, and it arched over the crossbar.

Kim had been beaten. She had taken the fake, and then she had made an awkward, off-balance stab at the ball. But somehow what she had done had worked.

She was both relieved and embarrassed.

But Franny was yelling, "Great job, Kim. You saved me. I don't think I could have stopped it."

Heather was yelling, "Kim, way to work. Good stop."

But it was the voice behind her that took Kim by surprise. "You're a bulldog, Kim. You don't give up."

Kim turned around and was looking at Allie. "I blew it. I let her get by me."

"Yeah. But you're so quick, you can make up for your mistakes."

"Sometimes."

"Well, just keep working as hard as you have been, and you're going to be a great player. When you first came out, I didn't think you would do that."

"I guess I didn't, either. I found out I *had* to."

Allie seemed ready to say something else, but the action was starting again and both girls had to get ready.

Kim was glad to see the Strider attack push the ball the other way. She didn't need any more pressure for a while. But she ran up the field and got in position to work with the attack. She had watched how hard Pam had kept going in spite of her injury, and Kim didn't want to do any less.

Not long after that, however, a Hurricane wing cut toward the goal. Marsella, trying to stay with her, banged into one of her own players. The wing broke into the goal area and got a great pass from one of the forwards.

Lorrie left her own mark, got to the girl, and made a good block. But she tripped the wing in the process, and the referee blew her whistle.

The ref awarded the Hurricanes a direct free kick. That meant Franny would be the only defender, and the forward would have a shot at the goal.

Franny set up for the block, and she even guessed right, diving to her left. But the shot was a real blast. It sliced away from Franny and into the corner of the net. There was no way she could have stopped it.

So the score was 1 to 1, and the Striders had themselves another tough match. It didn't matter to Kim who had made a mistake. The *team* had given up a score.

For some reason, though, Kim wasn't that worried. When the players walked off the field at halftime, they were tired, but Kim still had a good feeling about the way they were playing together. "We're going to win this one," she told Dawn. "We're playing like a team now. I can feel it."

The coach said basically the same thing. And she added something else. "We've got to keep the pressure on these kids. They don't have the depth we do. Their coach hardly substituted at all in the first half. Those girls have to be getting tired. I'm going to keep rotating all of you the way I did in the first half, and with our subs we don't lose much—maybe not anything. That should pay off for us in the second half."

It made sense. Fifteen strong players, not eleven. The subs were just as important as the starting players were. Kim had always said things like that. But now she knew it was true.

# CHAPTER
# 12

The second half started the way the first half had begun. The match was a hard-nosed defensive struggle—and Kim was on the sidelines. But before long, Kim could see the Striders getting the upper hand. Or at least they were the ones with the pressure on the Hurricane defense.

The problem was, they still needed to score.

Kim was yelling her voice hoarse, pushing her friends the only way she could for now. She had never made this much noise at any kind of game before, but she felt a need to be part of what was happening.

Kim whooped it up when the Striders got close a couple of times. And both times the team almost scored. Crystal missed a shot—barely wide—and the Hurricane goalie made a great stop on a good shot by Heather.

"Hey, we're getting there," Kim was yelling. "Pound it in the net next time. Keep the pressure on."

She was running up and down the field, along the touchline, to keep track of the action. She got a good look when Anne made a quick cut and stole a pass.

Anne tried to break away with the ball but got forced to the outside of the field. She couldn't get free to make a pass, or to center the ball, so she slowed and then dropped the ball back to Allie, who had come up behind her.

Allie dribbled the ball across the field while her defender stayed right with her. But she launched a long left-footed pass.

Kim was in awe of how most of the girls could kick as well with either foot. She just couldn't do that yet.

She was also impressed with the way Heather jumped for the pass and hit a header toward Crystal. It was hard to control a header and put it where it needed to go—but Heather made it happen. And Crystal darted to the ball.

She coiled back to fire a long shot, and Kim wondered what she was doing. But Crystal was only faking. She pushed a little pass toward Dawn, right in front of the goal area. Dawn's defender had also thought Crystal was going to shoot, and she had cut to the left.

That gave Dawn a little opening. She faced the goal and then nudged the ball ahead. She caught up with it just as the defense was closing in from both sides and the goalie was running forward.

Kim watched Dawn set her left foot and then twist her body around to the right as her leg came back like a sling. She stroked the ball hard, catching it with the inside of her foot. Her leg followed all the way through, and then she landed on the foot she had hit the ball with—exactly the way the coach taught the girls to do.

If the shot had been a few more inches to the left, the goalie could have blocked it. A few more inches to the right, and it would have sailed outside the goalpost. But it powered inside the goalpost and billowed the net with its force.

Kim forgot to yell. The picture she had just seen was too beautiful to shout about. It was just so perfect. All those years when Kim had been learning to play several sports, Dawn had centered on one, and she was a master at it. Kim had watched her play plenty of times, but that was before she had understood soccer enough to know what it took to be that good.

When Kim finally remembered to shout, she did plenty of it. And when she got back on the field to give Pam another rest, she played as though this were the championship match. The score was only

2 to 1, and she didn't want to let down and do something that would blow that narrow lead.

Her inexperience got her in trouble a couple of times, but her speed and determination saved her. And the Hurricanes didn't get another score.

When things got down to crunch time, and the Hurricanes were pulling out all the stops, the coach put Pam back in. That was fine with Kim. She went back to yelling and supporting.

And the coach's move paid off.

A Hurricane forward managed to break into the open, and she charged the goal. Pam saw what was happening and made a sudden move away from her mark, to cut off the forward. The forward tried to slip the ball back to the girl Pam had been covering, but she was too late. Shawndra had already seen that move coming and had rotated off her girl and over to the open player.

Shawndra knocked the ball away, and Pam, with her great balance, changed directions quickly and got to the ball first. She banged it out of the goal area, and a very serious threat was over.

Kim wondered. Would she have seen what to do soon enough? Would she have thought too long and not made the quick move to the other attacker in time? It was hard to say, but she knew why Pam was on the field now—when experience was needed.

As time was running down, the Hurricanes got just a little too intense about trying to score. Their defensive players were flooding in on the attack.

When Anne made a steal and booted the ball to Rachel, the Hurricanes couldn't get back on defense fast enough. Four Striders were running, passing, and moving the ball—and only two defenders were there to try to make the stop.

Kim could see that the Striders were keeping their heads. They drove hard, but they stayed under control, careful not to get an offside call, and they passed more than they dribbled.

Rachel broke to the goal from the wing and got a good pass from Allie. And Rachel had a shot. But she waited for the goalie to commit herself in her direction, and then she rolled the ball across the goal area in front of Crystal.

All Crystal had to do was run forward and bump the ball into the goal.

Crystal got the goal, but the whole team had gotten the score. It was a great thing to watch.

And that was it. The time ran out, and the Striders had the victory, 3 to 1. They were now 2 and 1 in the league, but more important, they were starting to click, starting to look like champions.

Kim ran onto the field as the game ended. She was trying to get to Dawn, but everyone ended up in a crowd—all the girls jumping on each other.

And Kim understood why. It wasn't just that they had won, but that they were playing so well together now. And they were feeling unified.

Somewhere in the middle of the chaos, Allie grabbed hold of Kim. "Come here," she said, pulling Kim out of the crowd. "Listen. There's something else I have to say to you."

Just then, someone—one of the player's mothers—grabbed Allie and told her what a great game she had played. It was something that Kim had experienced so many times, in other sports. But the woman only glanced at Kim and said, "You did a good job, too, honey."

Kim laughed as the woman walked away. So did Allie.

"She doesn't understand," Allie said. "She doesn't know how much you've learned. Honest. I've never seen anything like it. I thought you would quit after a couple of weeks. But you've worked your head off."

"I tried to quit," Kim said, and she laughed again. "The coach made me feel like a jerk, though."

"Well, anyway, you stuck, and I'm glad you did. And I'm sorry for some of the things I said."

"No big deal."

"Yeah, it is. I wasn't being fair. You're going to help us all season, even if you never start."

"Hey, I don't need to start. I just like playing a sport where everyone has to work so well together."

The coach was moving through the girls, congratulating them, and now she got to Kim and Allie. "Hey, you two, I'm glad to see you're talking to each other," she said. "Kim has come a long way, hasn't she?"

"She sure has. She's going to be a star," Allie said.

"No, no. I started too late. I just want to be the star of the second team."

"Hey, you already are," Allie said.

The coach put her arm around Kim's shoulder. "You played your heart out today," she said. "I was proud of you."

Afterward, when everything calmed down, Dawn and Kim finally had a chance to talk. "I didn't know how good you were until today," Kim said. "I finally know enough about the game so that I can understand."

"I'm just glad we can play together," Dawn said.

"Well, I'm glad I stayed with the team. I've learned some things."

"Isn't that what your dad told you would happen?"

Kim was surprised at the thought. "Oh, man, that's right. Hey, don't tell him I said that, okay? He loves to be right."

Dawn laughed. And then she looked over as her parents called to her.

"Do you want a ride home?" Dawn asked.

"No. I want to walk over to the softball field. The girls are practicing."

"Are you going to practice in your soccer uniform?"

"Oh…" Kim hesitated. But then she said, "Yeah, I think I will."

She knew she would have to listen to some sarcastic comments from her friends on the softball team. But right now, that really didn't bother her.

"You're never going to quit playing soccer now, Kim. You're hooked."

"Sooner or later, I'll have to choose," Kim said. "In high school, I won't be able to play softball and soccer at the same time."

"So which one do you think you'll play?"

"I don't know. Until today, that wasn't even a question. But now…I'm wondering."

Dawn was all smiles.

And Kim was stunned that she would hear herself saying such a thing. But she did like this game!

*The all-star soccer action starts here!*

# Angel Park
# SOCCER STARS™

*by Dean Hughes*

Jacob Scott is back with some new friends and a whole new sport—soccer. Join the Angel Park Pride as they pass, shoot, and score their way toward the league championship in an exciting series filled with the same nonstop action as the Angel Park All-Stars. You'll want them all for your collection!

**BULLSEYE BOOKS PUBLISHED BY RANDOM HOUSE, INC.**